1

<u>Believe it or Not by © "S.MANNAH"!!</u>

Copyright © Sweekriti Sethi 2018.

All Rights Reserved.

<u>*Prologue*</u>

My fascination towards writing and observing various things and individuals around me develops the habit of jotting down my zillion thoughts into fictional tales which are a part of the human life and the society we reside in. I pen down my own experiences and visions into fictional settings which are filled with flights of imagination and an undertone of intense message to be derived after reading from all the five senses and most importantly the heart, mind and the eternal soul. Yours truly ©*"S.MANNAH"*!! Copyright © 2019."S.MANNAH"!! The moral rights of the auth or has been asserted. All rights reserved. This story is published subject to the condition that it shall not be reproduced or retransmitted in whole or in part, in any manner, without the written consent of the copyright of this is a violation of copyright law. #shortstories #fictionwriters #microtales #flashfiction #storywritng #Horrortales #novella #novels #journal #poems #quotes.

Contents :-

~~~~~~~~~~~~~~~~~~~~~~~~~~~~~~~... ... ...
~~~~~~~~~~~~~~~~~~~~~~~~~~~~~~~

Believe it or Not by
©"S.MANNAH"!!

Each story focuses on a larger than life evil. It covers the entire realm of the supernatural- Ghosts, Ghouls, Goblins, Zombies, Haunted Houses, Ghost towns, Possessed objects, Witches & Wizards, Evil magicians, Revenge stories, Re-incarnation stories and much more than our mind can imagine!

Every house has a story. And some stories live on. Only to be re-lived by those who venture in. Creaking noises, footsteps, memories and nightmares, all are coming alive in our haunting tales of suspense, chills and thrills.

A collection of horror tales by "S.MANNAH"!!

Kindly Note:- We are not promoting or spreading Superstitions of any kind.

Disclaimer- All the characters and incidences depicted in this story are fictitious. Resemblance of any living or dead person is purely coincidental and unintentional...

It is a work of fiction.

(An Indian Hindi Horror Supernatural Thriller Anthology).

An anthology of horror tales by a fiction writer "S.MANNAH"!!

"One thing should be above all the religion of the world that is the religion of humanity"...

Gone are the days when the technologies has taken place and people have become more and more alienated from the personal touch of each other and had started to be interactive on the virtual world rather than being more warm and friendly through the gestures of meeting and greeting each other in person. Today's day and age are more interested in interacting through the social mediums such as WhatsApp, Facebook, Instagram, Snapchat, Tik-toks, Gmail,etc. which are created for the benefit of handling the long distance relationships of the social animals that is the human beings but with the rapid increase in the usage of Smartphone's somehow the warm personal touches that is friendly games, chats, gossips, storytelling arts have vanished due to the excessive usage and exposure of social media apps.

My aim is to not mislead anybody to not use or consume such helpful and useful application devices that is manufactured solely with the purpose of helping the masses to reach out to many more people of same interests, different wisdom and lifestyles but to remain intact with the roots of the Indian culture that is to remain in the close-knit circles of a group of people or a society that is coming together for a common motive that is to enlighten along with entertaining one and all but keeping the personal relations by meeting and greeting one another to share coming knowledge of the past, present and the future for their forthcoming generations.

India is a land of so many cultures and its roots are formed by the art of tale-telling that is the sharing of cultural stories, myths, folk legends that covers a large part of the folklore comprises in the Indian continent. My sole purpose is to unite the bonds of people in the age-old manner with the help of storytelling by word of mouth that will be remembered as a part of folktales of our own Indian continent and it's rich culture of encompassing disparate stories that is remarkable in adoring the rich Indian culture and it's ancient art of storytelling for fun, frolic and enlightenment of the soul. One such genre of literature as well as folk-culture that is been adored by many people together whether in forming chill down their spines or by giving them goose-pimples after reading or listening them is none other than the Horror stories that compels everybody to sit together in a group circle and narrate either their paranormal experiences or a known legend or a horror folktale that is been shared by the word of mouth medium that obviously forms a rich folktale anthology collection of selective thriller tales and occult mysteries which is generally beyond the reach of an average human mind. In either cases it is something personal and had to do with the beliefs of people to trust on such unknown entities such as ghosts, vampires, witches, werewolves, wizards, spooks, spectres of evil or kind spirits, strange occurrences & happenings, fantasy & supernatural or mysterious stories, trickster tales, etc. that obviously forms a paranormal cluster of mysticism and also people that posses the mystic powers.

There is a page on the social media Messenger site like Facebook with the title of ***"(Bhoot Aaya) Do Not Enter Near the Sun"*** for some enthusiasts, paranormal investigators and religious readers of mystery & supernaturally occult and horror tales from around the world by the word of mouth of people from all walks of life that unites a small community of some people together. Together they forms a secret society of enthu-cutlets who are interested in knowing or discovering the unknown entities that exists within all of us but only can be sensed and viewed by few psychic and mystic people who has the potential to see beyond the knowledge and sensory power of the human mind. The main folks entering the group with a common desire to share some personal experiences, some ommon knowledge and mory of some heard & unheard stories were namely 1*Mouli Ganguli, 2Rajkumar Nigam, 3Krystle Reddy, 4 Gulshan Soni,* 5Kiku Grover, 6Vicky Tandon and couple 7*Enna & Dushyant Sarkar who had* befriend each other through teh help of Facebook a social media site page ***"Do Not Enter Near the Sun"*** for the common purpose of sharing such tales with each other as they are extremist s who were extremely fond of knowing something unknown and mystical. They all decides to meet up on every Saturday midnight at a location which is alienated □ □ to get that spooky and eerie touch because they are all extremists and believer in the occult sciences that is beyond the sensory vision and understanding of the average human being. It is kind of sadistic pleasure they derived to torture themselves by visiting that haunting kind of strange and bizarre location that is named ***"Mohini Bagh"*** which is named after a princess *Mohini* who has died a miserable death of isolation and has been often addressed in the folktales as a schizophrenic patient who can see the realm of ordinary human visions and perceptions as she often claims. Some folktales suggests that she has committed suicide by hanging herself by a banyan tree that is situated outside her palace's ***Shringar Kothi's*** huge garden. Some stories claims that it is the deed of some unknown supernatural and mystical entity that has possessed ***Mohini,*** while some legends says that ***Mohini*** died due to the asphyxia condition due to insufficient & deficient supply of oxygen needed for natural breathing by an average human being to survive on the planet earth under natural circumstances. But the mystery of her death always remains a mystery, a long silenced secret that remained a secret forever.

The mansion has become a living example of a deserted and a jinxed place due to the princess's mysterious death at such a n early age that is 21 years old. The palace has been cursed and it is often advised by people residing in that location to never visit the place after 8 O'clock in the night as the ghost of *Mohini* often visits the place and dances and merry-makes by producing a peculiar sound of her anklets that has been heard by many people of the village and the sound of the wind of that place is also extremely creepy because of low density and extreme wild greenery. The palace is somewhat 200 miles away from *New Delhi.*

All the friends unite every Saturday as they plans a weekend getaway from the regular and mundane hullabaloo of life to share some interesting folktales which they knew it they are aware of which they may have heard from someone once in their lifetime or may have experienced by their own senses once in a blue moon as such experiences are in the destiny of very few chosen ones. Thus all the companions as excellent storytellers unites and reunites on every 2nd weekend of Saturday to share a paranormal and occult story that is stored as a part of their memory with others for the common motive of entertainment and love for hearing horror and gruesome mystical tales that chills down their spines at every second weekend night ☐ at the deserted and lonely land of **Mohini Bagh**.

The friends met as planned on the first chilling nights of cold-icy December night at around 11:55 p.m. and started narrating their first story by the word of mouth. The first narrator of the story is *Gulshan Soni* who has a very interesting story to tell to everyone of them in the full moon forever silenced mysterious night. But before beginning the tale all have collectively and mutually rechristened the session of storytelling into *Crescent Moon*☐ a title suggested by *Mouli Ganguly* the fearless and rebellious out of all present out there in the most cherish able night.

Storytelling 1.0 : Title- Ghode ki Naal

It was the era before the partition of India and Pakistan this first story is by *Gulshan Soni*. *Gulshan's* granny narrated him a bizarre horror tale every evening of Sunday when he does oils her granny's hairs and does her new hairstyles and in return he gets the treasure of listening beautifully concocted tales equipped with suspense, thrills and chills of spine chilling experiences. *Sheela Sawhney's* mother *Nirmals's parents* Saroj and husband *Melaram and Sheela Ji's late grandparents were* going back to Lahore, Pakistan from Pulwama, Kashmir and to reach the place fast as they had reached the city but to reach *Lahore's Fatehabad road Mehtab Bagh* where they used to live at that time.

In order to reach the place they hired a tanga wala that is a horse cart as that is predominantly was the mode of transportation at that time. As there was a strike of passenger transports during the tension between the two borders that is before 1947 scene and lifestyle the only horse cart that gets ready to drop *Gulshan's* granny *Sheela's* grandparents (*Saroj & Melaram*). *They* got ready to settle on the cart as they were in a hurry but the bizarre thing that they had discovered is that the tangawala does not ride the horse cart properly maybe because he seems heavily sozzled. *Saroj ji* asks him to run the cart on slow pace as she is getting scared that they will definitely met with an accident if he keeps riding like in his usual bizarre style. But the cart puller does not listen to her warnings and keeps riding in the same manner so much so that he even gets paranoid that if she keeps annoying him like that then he will leave them (couple) in the middle of the road. As the spouse were left with no other option and the fact that the route is very isolated due to the emergency crisis and riots and all that also took place at irregular intervals so they both mutually decided to not argue with the tangawala and continued their journey.

At some distance the tangawala stopped his horse cart and reached near a Banyan tree☐ and within no time he climbed the tree to catch a mud pot that is tied up the tree. Both the spouse were highly distressed and petrified as both were regretting to sit on his cart because they were suspecting him to be a hooligan or a thug or might be terrorist that will kill them in search of more money and to satiate his sadistic desires. But if they reacted then the old couple will be in trouble as the man can get really aggressive by nature because he already seem drunk like hell. *Saroj & Lala Melaram* saw that the cart puller picked up a round mud pot from the branches of a tree that is tied together over top of the tree and after coming down on the earth he drank something from the clay pot which seems really unusual and frightening. It was a kind of desi daru means it was alcohol that is termed as desi tharra/Tahari a local national drink which is extremely intoxicating and it affects the mind like a strong drug which both the couple are aware of really well. Both are now afraid even more as they worry that how can a cart puller ride the horse cart by consuming so much more alcohol over already been heavily drunk earlier as it is reflected in his stuttering speeches and staggering walks.

Saroj and *Melaram* decided to pay the cart puller his fees and to leave the horse cart but the cart puller refuses to leave them in the middle of the road as he has promised to drop them towards their residence as a passenger destination. Without any further arguments the cart puller continues riding the horse cart and this time he rides 1000 times faster than before as a repercussion of the highly intoxicating desi alcohol that affects the mind rapidly after consuming it and the consumer became highly energetic and in the effect of the alcohol can do anything as the mind is not in his hands anymore but in the absolute control of the alcohol. The man rides as fast as he can with a swift and rapid speed that almost took the couple's breat away but finally they reached their pavilion after some time. *Saroj* and *Melaram* took a sigh of relief after reaching finally to their destination as soon as they had stepped out of the cart they took out the fees of the tangawala in order to pay him the charge of the ride of the transport facility of the horse cart/ ghoda gaadi. But when the lady was about to give the money that is □20 to the tangawala she shouted out loud in shock and fear. The reason for her agonising scream was due to the tangawala that has a strange and bizarre looking hands as his hands are replaced by the horse hands that is the horse's front legs which is extremely grotesque, gruesome, horrendously horrifying and terrifying for the senses to view it with the naked eyes that appears like a horseshoe.

The End...

Storytelling 2.0:_ Title - <u>Let the Puppets Speak~Kathamrita Returns.</u>

The second story was narrated by *Vicky Tandon* that was a real-life incidence that has took place in his own hometown many years ago. Once upon a time in the *Gokul Pura* location of *Agra* in the year 1990 a popular incident has been reported that has shell-shocked and flabbergasted one and all whosoever has heard it or read it in the local news papers like *Amar Ujala, Dainik Jagran, DLA, Kalptaru*, Desi Patrika, Hindustan and the like. The news has shook the senses of many people like never before was one of the talk of the town at that time. This is an incident that took place in the **'*Maya Niwas'*** where the entrance walls were decorated by Rajasthani puppets that has the power to speak in the midnight and early morning at 4 o'clock. The scenes opens when two beautiful puppets named *Radha Krishna* were talking to each other and telling the other two puppets *Shiva Parvati* about the heroic deeds of the two companions *Veera* aka *Kathamrita* and her friendly dog *Hero.* The girl has scolded some hooligan boys of her locality whose names were main culprit *Raja, Keshav, B.Lal, Ashish* who often disturbs others by their mischievous behaviour and every people wanted to get rid of the local goons, thugs and thieves that has become havoc for the localities of that alley.

One day the perpetrators and eve-teasers *Raja, Lakhan, B.Lal, Abu Sheikh, Ashish, Keshav* started throwing stones and huge brick pieces on the dogs and especially small and little puppies of the stray doggies on order to trouble them and kill them a sadistic and agonising death to satiate their sadistic and disturbed psychologically ill & sick desires. They have an excuse that the dogs used to bite them and also bark at them whenever they pass by from the residence of *Kathamrita aka Veera* that is **Maya Niwas.** When *Kathamrita* stopped the perpetrators from commuting this sinful deed of troubling in the paradise of the poor stray animals so they all molesters and rascals started abusing and badmouthing *Kathamrita* only and seeing this sight *Hero* cannot contain his emotion as he angrily and aggresively pounced upon the hooligans which heated up the situation. Somehow *Veera* aka *Kathamrita* abstains *Hero* from doing it and some people handled the situation by making the hooligans go away from that spot but this argument and rift will only be increased afterwards and not going to be put to rest.

When the Ganghor ka Mela took place in the *Balka Basti, Kansa Gate, Thandi Sadak.* The whole lane of *Gokul Pura* was empty as all houses were isolated because all of the residents had gone to the religious Mela/Fair except *Kathamrita* who was not too well so she had planned to visit the spiritual ad devotional Mela the next day. But at around 12 O'clock whn she came out to feed some roti dipped with dhoodh to the stray animals like dogs and cows she discovered the same hooligan boys *Raja, B. Lal, Abu Sheikh, Ashish And Keshav* who were waiting to teach *Kathamrita stopped a lesson* by hitting her with a huge and heavy stick on her head's sensitive part in order to kill her and the advantage was that they spotted her outside the *Gokul Pura* locality all alone and timidly feeble and the benefit wa that the whole town is busy in the celebration of **Ganghor Mela** that is a celebration where Hindu god and goddess that is *Gaura and Parvati* were married in a ritual ceremony with bright colours and grand feasting as the people rejoice in the prayers, chanting and indulges into grand food, swings and shopping various traditional and cultural stuff from the fair/ mela.

When *Kathamrita* was leaving the road o enter her residence *Maya Niwas* from her backside the sadist and hooligan *Raja* attacked *Kathamrita urf/aka Veera* from a huge stick that hit her head so hard that she died on the spot due to brain haemorrhage accident. When *Hero* cake he spotted that *Kathamrita* wa spying unconscious on the ground as *Hero* the dog has gone to the other gali/ lane that is the *Khinni Gali* to meet his siblings so he was unaware of the event but soon the pious dog figures out what has happened with his beloved friend *Kathamrita aka Veera bhen.* He felt extremely apologetic and guilty of not being present at the time the attack took place and obviously the culprits had eloped away after committing the sinful deed of murdering *Kathamrita. Hero* figures out with the help of his sixth sense, his divine powers the cause of *Kathamrita's* early and forcefully unwanted demise that the unnecessary demand se occured dur to the culprits *Raja, B.Lal, Lakhan, Ashish, Keshav* and gang. *Hero* immediately went towards the small temple situated at the *Mansa Devi Gali* of *Kali Mata Rani* who is known to destroy the evil powers. The goddess *Kali* understands his woes and pangs for his beloved human friend *Kathamrita* and she blesses the dog with immense powers and energy to perniciously destroy *Raja and gang* because it is very important to support goodness over the evil alto bring equality to teach the masses the concept of the victory/ triumph of good over the evil and in this task he is befriended with other dog army of heavenly dogs and none other than the spirit of *Kathamrita. Goddess Kali* by her divine powers and manifestation shows her giant reflection and also makes the dead body of *Kathamrita* invisible and locked her house residence **Maya Niwas.**

After the Oracle of goddess *Kali* stops speaking a voice is heard in the air and it ©was none other than the vocals of *Kathamrita aka Veera* who has descended on the earth for the unconditional love of brave and a dedicated friend *Hero.* The spirit of *Kathamrita* returns to meet *Hero* and together they decide to put an end to the torture of the evil minded people that had burdened the Mother Earth. The Ganghor Mela will take place for the 3 consecutive nights and the whole crowd will be gathered into the ground where the ceremony will take place and as usual the hooligans *Raja, Ashish, Keshav, B.Lal, Abu Sheikh after getting heavily* drunk in the night. As planned all the drunkards came towards the **Maya Niwas.** The obnoxious monsters came to plunder *Kathamrita's* house as they had thought that the society peoplez; citizens must have burned her into ashes as she has died. But when they went towards the residence **Maya Niwas** they were left gobsmacked after seeing the main gate was pad-locked. *Raja* asks his fellow hooligan companions to give him the same stick with which they had attacked *Kathamrita* the last night. But when he was about to hit the lock of the main gate in order to open it various deadly, aggressive and wild dogs came running towards the bastards and charge an attack towards them like a wild wild predator.

The last attack was made by *Hero* towards *B.Lal, Abu Sheikh, Keshav, Ashish and all of them died a painful and terrible death by the deadly and fatal bites of the brutally wild animals.* Except *Raja* all the scoundrels had died a miserable & merciless death. *Hero* went towards *Raja* who was thinking and perceiving it as a nightmare. *It's time for Hero to font ut out on a one on one level. Hero expresses through his gestures* to fight out with him in order to make it into an equal battle but *Raja* was not powerful enough to defeat him except his overconfidence and obnoxious ego. This time with the last blow by *Hero the brave dog he was* accompanied by *Kathamrita but as she does not have a* bhotik/ physical body she cannot touch or beat *Raja but in return she asks Hero to kill this dirt on Earth that has not only killed and tortures several people but has also burdened the* Mother Earth that even the goddess Mother Earth wanted to get rid of such selfish and obnoxious creep from her surface. Thus with his last massive and thunderous clout/ punch/blow Hero finishes the chapter of *Raja forever as after being attacked Raja fell off the ground like a withering leaf from the tree. This marks the end of the terrorism of Raj and gang along with the message of teaching the masses about the difference between the good path as well as th bad path in life. "No matter how much the bad path* becomes humongous and supreme but it'll always remain a micro particle in front of the goodness in people or the good or the wise path. Thus after finishing their tale the two puppets *Radh*a and *Krishna ends their storytelling* narration with a loud laugh and they didn't forget to mention the climate of that time that matches with the rainy season of the current time. The other two puppets *Shiva* and *Parvathy* surprisingly about the abouts of *Kathamrita* and *Hero after th*e battle with the evil forces and what has happened with the heavenly dogs after all? *Radha Krishna puppets* winded up their journey of *Kathamrita and her loyal buddy Hero and their undying immortal love and admiration for each other by describing that after killing the monstrous Raja the whole sky gets darker and with a roaring thunderous sound effect produced by the clouds up above the sky Goddess Kali* invokes and blesses *Hero.* After sometime all the other dog companions who are the descendants of the heavenly abode disappeared. After successfully accomplishing the task of taking revenge from the culprit *Raj*a *the Goddess Kali akss Katha aka* Veera to join her to the heavenly abode as her time period has been over from the planet Mother Earth and it is time for the new journey to get started.

But *Hero* cannot digest the fact of parting away from his beloved dear friend *Kathamrita, therefore he requested the mother like goddess to grant Kathamrita her life back but that cannot happen because once the time period is over then willingly or unwillingly one has to shed their physical form* to manifest into a transcendental form of no boundaries that is the spiritual manifestation as it is predestined in the destiny of *Kathamrita* that her life on the earth will be short-lived but still it will be full of didactic lessons and complesion. *Kathamrita* convinces *Hero to make her leave for the betterment of everyone but took a promise from the loyal stray dog to* use her residence for the betterment of humankind and for the welfare of the society and its inhabitants who need healings and solace from ignorance to bliss. *Hero* promises her to always protect and to look after her residence and to convert it into an NGO for the really needy poor kids for their further education and for the sustainance of all the stray dogs as they too need a home like any other human being or a pedegreed dog. Looking at their eternal and unconditional feelings for each other the statue of motherhood and motherly emotions *Goddess Kali grants Hero to see his believed dear friend Kathamrita whenever he misses or needs her the most in his quest to establish humanity in the world* full of hatred and pessimistic negativity only to establish humanity in general.

The citizens never got to know the truth they only got to know that *Raja* was invoked in the disappearance of *Kathamrita* who never was found again by anyone as she was also an orphan. For *Raja* a very famous story got circulated that die to his immense tortures of poor souls of humans and animals he was punished a painful death by the almighty that has an invisible register of each and everyone's Karma/ deeds which will be judged whenever the torture of the human population rises above the sea level. That will be done by the court that is above all the honorary courts of law and justice that is the court of the Supreme Lord that is the whole Universe. Believe it or not but some stories are considered beautiful because there is no end to it or there's still a hint of riddle left to their completion says *Radha the puppet while hanging on the wall while the* other three puppets *Krishna, Shiva and Parvathy* stared with contentment and a surprised face to the narrator of *Kathamrita returns. The last scene of the story ended by showing Kathamrita herself in the form of a* spirit alongwith Hero who only has the power to see her beloved dear friend while the NGO kids *Monika and ot*hers were reading Indian Mythological stories along with many dogs friends and parrots, pigeons, cow, buffalo, horse, bats, cats were sitting along with them and greenery is present all around. While the kids reads the numerous stories and the animals rejoices it was shown that both *Kathamrita and Hero was seen giving a mischievous look ad* smile of contentment towards the end. The end of the fantastical folktale shows the front side of the residence of *Kathamrita* that has been rechristened as ***Maya Niwas NGO for the orphans and Animals.***

The End...

Storytelling 3.0:- Title- Hourglass

The third story was narrated by *Krystle Reddy* about a girl from *Nirvana Kunj, Delhi* named *Harshdeep Somya Kaur*. In the morning she woke up around 8:30 a.m. and got ready to reach her designer boutique **Atharva Pehnawa** as she is an entrepreneur by profession. Before going to her boutique she met her family that is her mother *Inderpreet Kaur, father Jaspal Singh* Bhatti and younger sister *Aakanshi Kaur and her beautiful 6 pet birds and animals that is 4 dogs Ginger, Toffee, Candy, Cola and 2 parrots Mishthi and Rana*. She bid all of them goodbye before leaving to her designer boutique in her WagonR car towards the route *Gailana Road, Kailash Parwat* where her **Atharva Pehnawa** *boutique is built up.* While driving her car she encountered various scenes on the road such as early morning children going to their schools on the school buses, the jalebi kachori market which is getting open in the morning, the passengers hurriedly settling themselves in the passengers vehicles such e-rickshaws, city buses, CNG auto-rickshaws, etc. to reach their working places like offices, college, and the like. *Harshdeep Somya Kaur* encountered and captured lot many moments on the road and all the hullabaloo of the society and its daily working to sustain a lifestyle. She also saw a baloon wala, a cotton candy wala and a sugar candy wala selling their products for kids and all.

Suddenly she saw a beautiful and strangely alluring dreamcatcher that a man is selling on the *Hariparwat footpath along with some decorative birds nests for the living* & drawing rooms. Immediately after getting attracted by the magnificent charm of the dreamcatcher *Harshdeep* purchased the dream-catcher for her boutique as she is fond of collecting windchimes, and fancy things like such for the aim of decorating her boutique and house with such beautiful collection if different items. She asked the seller/vendor to give her the dreamcatcher as it provides delight and positive vibes to hang on the wall of her boutique **Atharva Pehnawa.** *"Rajpal hai mera naam", says the vendor and showed Harshdeep her choice of dreamcatcher that is white and purple in colou*r. After getting her favourite dream-catcher she went straight to the *Gailana Road, Khadi* Market where her designer boutique was situated and after reaching the boutique she instantly hanged the dream-catcher on the nail that is at the middle of the boutique. She is fond of such items and also antique items. *Harshdeep Somya* has a beautiful hourglass as well that is kept at her working table where she used to sit in her boutique shop. After sometime of settling on her chair she saw all the orders that has been left and also ready to be given to the customers/clients.

Some 4 customers came and given their orders while 2 have come to get their already done orders of blouses and traditional suits with Nakashi and Kadhai with a modern touch to it given as a fusion. After sometime *Harshdeep Somya* realises a slight change in her skin and complexion that appears withered from her both hands. When she saw herself in the mirror she was left flabbergasted, she was left extremely stumped and speechless as she felt that the ground is slipping under her feet. She has become old, haggered and withered like an old human being in the age group of 50-55 years. Thus sight has stupified *Harshdeep Somya* and she started to bewilder about the strange circumstance that has occured in her life as she was alright in the mirror when she saw herself in her residential mirror but now she looks old and withered like a falling leaf from the tree whose charm and youth has gone forever. In order to confirm she also views her face in her mobile camera and in that also her face appears old and wrinkled but a strange and bizarre thing that she has spotted in her mobile phone was the present year that shows 2040 from 2019 that is a long leap which *Harshdeep* us unable to understand as according to her she is just 28 years old who is soon going to be 29 years old in the month of December. The strange and weird phenomenon took her senses like never before. At that time her friend *Jasveer Kaur* came to meet her in her boutique who has also become wrinkled beauty with old age with 2 children *Chunnu Munnu* as she carries her children with her and starts calling them with that name. *Harshdeep* asks her friend *Jasveer* about the strange incidence that has happened with both of them as she is assuming it a disease attack or something. She said, "*Look at us what has* happened *to both of us why are we looking so tired, wrinkled, timid and* haggard, where has our youth disappeared?"

Jasveer Kaur told her that we have grown up so gracefully then what the heck you at talking have you lost it or something, it this a kind of memory losee or something like an partial anterograde amnesia or something just so silly and ignorent. *Jasveer* told her that it is indeed 2040 and not 2019 you are talking of that golden years have passed so gracefully and brilliantly. This has left *Harshdeep* gobsmacked and she is not able to digest this sudden revelation by her perpetual senses. She wished to talk to *Maraj her* tailor in the boutique **Atharva** Pehnawa but as *Jasveer* told *Harshdeep* that *Maraj* has ran away some 10 years ago to *Dubai* due to some fraud he has committed in India by plundering so many people in the name of a committee he has opened to earn easy monthly investments for gaining more and more money. His treachery was caught and he was left with no other option but to run away from India in order to save his life from the goons and people who are after his life for their rented money, since then he has not contacted anyone from.his known contacts in order to change his identity due to the scam he has committed in India. *Harshdeep is unaware of everything that Jasleen has* narrated to her about *Maraj* and couldn't remeber anything in her memory she continues thinking and uttering that she is in the 2019 era and remember that her friend is unmarried with no young boys of such good age. She wished to call her good childhood friend *Aadil Uddin but* again she is stopped by *Jasveer* as she revealed to her that she has forgotten everything and everyone or must have completely gone bonkers by the disorder of *retrograde* amnesia. *Jasveer* told her that *Aadil* has left India to settle in LA some 5 years ago as he got good job opportunity there and also married some foreigner there to acquire permanent citizenship of the country after having 2 children *Reem and Ibrahim.* *Jasveer* advised *Harshdeep* to take a day's rest by shutting the shop today and relax for sometime by taking proper rest as she seems stressed out. Having said that she left to her residence building with her boys. At the same time *Harshdeep closes her boutique **Atharva Pehnawa*** by locking it and rushed towards her residence **Gulmohar Grand.** While driving she encountered the same scenaries and scenarios, the cotton candy seller, the same greenery, the Mithai seller, the flower vendor, the Golgappe vendor, the deities and temples but not the man *Rajpal from whom she has bought the dreamcatcher.* When she reached her house she parked her car and went inside the house by opening the gate with the extra smart key that she has with her.

But she was left surprised as she didn't find anyone in the house as she keeps calling all her family with their names, *Maa, Papa, Aakanshi also all her 6 pets but she was unable to find anyone in the house. The strange part is that nobody used to be out at that time but that day nobody was* inside the house which baffles *Harshdeep Somya Kaur and it seems extremely bewitching and* unbelievable. When she tries calling on her parents joint phone number the voice says that the dialled number does not exist and same for her sister's mobile number. But there are two SIM numbers of *Aakanshi* and immediately *Harshdeep* contacted in the second number to know about the whereabouts of everyone from her as she is unable to understand the whole situation on her own, it almost seem like an unsolved puzzle to her in which she gets trapped by any mafia gang or something mystic that she is unable to interpret and understand by her own mind and senses.

The call was picked by a man who claims to be *Aakanshi's husband Dilpreet Singh Tuteja* who gives phone to *Aakanshi in order to talk to her elder sister Harshdeep.* When *Harshdeep asked* what is happening in the family how do you get married and why isn't she knowing anything about it, if this a kind of prank then this is of the worst kind?

*Aakansh*i told her sister that she must be daydreaming as as it has been many years since she is married to Dr. *Dilpreet Singh Tuteja* and both their parents have passed away many many years ago as well as their beloved pets and it is now just both the sisters who are left as a family but she cannot come to her because her in-laws and husband does not allow her to come to meet her elder sister that is *Harshdeep said Aakanshi.* She disconnected the call abruptly as her husband starts scolding her while she was talking to her sister for a long time on the phone. This baffles *Harshdeep* and she started crying out loud due to losing her whole family and been left alone as a spinster. She saw her face in the mirror and cried her heart out as she misses her whole family like so badly. She sat on the floor of her house putting her head down while she keeps crying indefinitely as all her silent suppressed emotions were keep exploding uncontrollably. Suddenly a loud voice was heard that spreads in the air explosively that made *Harshdeep Somya Kaur to wake up with fear and she realises that she was on her bed and bla*nket and she was dreaming all this while about all such events that took place in her life but the twist of the matter is that it was a dream and not reality. She took sigh of relief after uniting with her beloved pets who came to greet her *Good* Morning. *Harshdeep Somya got a bit calm and* patient after seeing her parents and sister roaming around the room all hale and hearty.

The End...

©*"S.MANNAH"!!*

(All Rights Reserved).

Storytelling 4.0 ~ Title- "Incense Sticks"...

The fourth story has been narrated by _Kiku Grover on Saturday midnight to all his friends in_ **Mohini Bagh** when all United for a common motive to hear bizarre and incredibly mystic and paranormal stories as well as experiences. This story has been his (_Kiki's_) personal experience when he was 17 years old, when he and his family that consists of mother _Veena Grover_, father _Suraj Grover, and younger sister Suratpriya Gr_over all have shifted to the location _Naglahaveli House no. 7/77. Everything went out quite well until_ Thursday 13th 2018 when some strange incidences took place in their house such as some voices were heard like the sound of ghungroo, the windows were constantly been shut and opened on its own despite of no wind flowing and the windows were locked with the stopper but somehow it gets open on its own.

Some distance away from _Naglahaveli a Dargah is located that is Abu Lala ki Dargah which is infamous for warding off the ev_il energies and powers such as the evil spirits and possessed demons out of the body of the victims those were troubled by the mischievous spirits of the evil ghouls and the demonic spirits those were stuck on the earth and is in search of a physical body so they keep on possessing humans that has high chances of getting possessed by spirits and ghosts. _Suratpriya_ used to lighten some aromatic Incense stick that are perfumed with beautiful scent which spreads positivity and dense fragrance in every corner of the ro where it is placed. The incense sticks are of _Mogra aroma that is available from a nearby grocery_ shop. The paranormal activities suspected in the house no.7/77 were not new as the family of _Kiku_ was told by their neighbours that before them 17 people have left this house by suspecting and encountering some strange and bizarre events that are occult, mysterious, thrilling and full of mystical elements. Some neighbours also claims that this house was once owned by a man who has died some 100 years ago after committing suicide or some stories says that the man whose name is _Ranchodh Kumar Dutta died by battling depression as his adopted son and his family alienated him in this house and in the grief_ of their separation he does in his old age when he was 90 years old but his spirit never really left the earth and keeps haunting the inhabitants of this cursed house no.7/77 as many people have reported haunting and unexplainable incidences that are too haunting and terrifying for the senses. The petrified 17 people never really dared to come back again in this petrifying cursed house.

The neighbours give advice to the _Grover's_ to visit the _Peer Baba_ to ward off the evil from their house or if it is possible then vacate the house as it is not suitable for living. When the sufferers went to the _Abu Lala ki Dargah they saw that the people were acting weird over there as they are abnormally doing somersaults and climbing up a giant and huge tree without_ waiting for even a second. The place is full of negative energy as it is covered by the celestial energies of the paranormal surroundings and energies. The ghost catcher was sent to the family by the _Molana ji from the Dargah to stop the terrorism of the nasty spirit_ of _Ranchodh._ But the spirit refuses to leave his residence and is adamant to stay eternally as his soul is attached with his house. The paranormal investigator investigated that the Incense Sticks of the _Mogra aroma attracted the ghost of Ranchodh who has lost his_ physical manifestation and is now currently a spirit that is stuck in the twilight kingdom due to unfulfilled desires in his humanly manifestation. The ghost of _Ranchod_h went inside the pious _Mogra_ Incense Sticks who has been inside it and by the supernatural and divine powers the paranormal expert mystic catches the ghost inside a tiny glass bottle and he took it with him to the Dargah where a huge tree is standing that has some sly and pawky spirits tied on small and tiny glass bottles which were tightly been locked and hold with a thread chanted by some Tantra Mantra by the mystic *Peer Baba. Finally the Grover's were* relieved from the dangerous and stubborn ghost of *Ranchodh. But Veena Grover has decided to leave the house as she is not convinced with the idea of stayi*ng in a haunting house like such so the whole family has shifted to *New Kaveri Kunj road and tried to forget everything that happened with them in the house no.*7/77 . From that day onwards the house was permanently closed and nobody has purchased the house after the *Grover's as they were the last inhabitants of that jinxed haunted residence. Therefore it will be their first session of autobiographical paranormal and supernatural* storytelling night.

The End...

©*"S.MANNAH"!!*

Storytelling 5.0~ Title- Mystery is yet to be Revealed.

Rajkumar Nigam has an interesting and different set of takes to rejoice in the next Saturday. He has a unique set of tales from *Lucknow, Uttar Pradesh,* the Indian culture and it's rich roots of storytelling through the Indian puppeteers and Indian Rajasthani style puppet arts that narrates various cultural and mythical stories in the form of folktales, folksongs, folk music, folkdances that is a common art in India. It is said that when Goddess *Parvati* got angry with Lord *Shiva in order to impress and make Parvati ji happy Lord Shiva gets inside a puppet and performs dances in order to persuade the* beautiful goddess. However, it is indeed very ironical that the richest Indian culture is now vanishing, fading away as the government not the people takes any interest in its original and incredible way of storytelling through the medium of puppet art that narrates bizarre, humorous and colourful stories from all walks of life to the people for their entertainment and enlightenment to their soul and also pleasurable for their senses and worth cherishing for their neosis.

Once a very famous theatre **Mayuri Puppet Theatre (Kathputli Khel Tamasha)** in Lucknow, Uttar Pradesh showcases beautiful storytelling of *Mahabharata, Ramayana, Vikram Betal tales, Rana Pratap tales, Prithviraj Chauhan tales, Akbar Birbal tales, Panchatantra tales, Tenali Raman tales of* wit and wisdom, etc. by the word of mouth two prominent central characters, protagonists **Gulabo Sitabo** *who is also a part of the Indian folktales that the two puppets were Sautans; co-wife of a man that has been circulated by word of mouth storytelling art many many years ago from now like centuries ago most probably. Gulabo Sitabo's main voice was actually the mastermind that keeps this Indian* culture alive was a man named *Manno* who used to tie up the puppets on the *Gulmohar* tree and then gets them down and makes them perform as he is a ventriloquist who becomes the voice of both *Gulabo and Sitabo.*

Gulabo and Sitabo started fighting as Sautans like usually they share a love-hate relationship and never agreed on a point and always ends up quarrelling with each other on various issues and topics and discussions. Meanwhile in between *Ganesha* provides background music.

Part 1:- Pernicious Encounters.

Gulabo started addressing the crowd present in the theatre with her grandma's Sitamai's tale that she was told in her childhood by the mouth of her beloved granny *Sitamai. She told everyone as well as Sitabo that the tale is about her grandmother's childhood time when she was barely 8 years old. They were 7 younger siblings, 1 younger sister and 5 younger brothers. She* was carrying her toddler brother who was just birn child and infant only as her mother *Kartaro Devi told Sitamai to go out with all her siblings to buy some fruits.*

While in the meanwhile *Sitamai* encountered a strange looking women who is weird and gorgonish as she is mysterious and dark from every angle but in a negative sense. The lady called the gullible girl *Sitamai* towards her who is carrying her infant baby brother *Bholu . The* innocent girl cannot understand the evil and ulterior motives of the evil lady who addressed herself as *Lowleen. The lady Lowleen saw the baby and touches the* baby for some time and wished to carry the baby in his arms but *Sitamai refuses to give her baby as mother has taught her to not trust* strangers and this infuriated the sly lady she looked at the baby with some strange looking reddish eyes full of fury and anger. After this *Sitamai* went to her house that is in *Rawalpindi, Pakistan.*

After reaching her house the family registered some strange incidence that took place with the new born baby that is *Bholu.* Some blue coloured saliva came out of *Bholu's* mouth and suddenly he gets unconscious. When the *Hakim* ji arrived he declared him dead and lifeless on the spot. *Alas! The poor child has passed* away. When *Sitamai* was inquired about the cause of his death as the last person who was with *Bholu who was matured also was Sitamai only.* Her younger brother *Nikhar* told his parents that the lady from the *Dayalbagh's Prem Niwa*s called out *Sitamai* and also touches *Bholu. Sitamai* also mentioned the same thing that has happened some hours ago. *The mother has broken down completely but the neighbours informed the family that the lady was of a questionable morale and she is infamous for performing black magic on children and on people. She has the power to hypnotise anyone by her sorcery. She is a barren, a sterile woman, a childless lady who was also thrown out of her husband's house because of her black art that* uses for disturbing and manipulating others for her own vested interests. Although it is bad to state such superstitious things about women but the results and people encounter as well as personal experiences, interactions states these thoughts about the lady *Lowleen.* The lady is always jealous with married people and especially those who have beautiful and healthy looking kids. The story serves as a message to the society in lot many ways about people's psychology and mindsets also it is is important to understand to not let small children take such big responsibility of their younger siblings at such a tender age. But whatever happened will be a big mystery as the child loses his life due to poison that was injected in his body that supposedly magically with the help of sorcery been given to the infant by the sorceress. But whatever is the real matter this tale has also ended abruptly without a logical end and conclusion.

The End...

Part 2:- <u>Crossdressing.</u>

After hearing the haunting tale of *Gulabo, Sitabo* also narrated a tale from her hometown *Neemuch, Madhye Pradesh* when she was 14 years old she has two friends who were sisters named *Tanvi Yashvi* who resides at *Mansa Devi Gali community* and *Sitabo before marriage always goes to meet her friends at their home in the evening.* One day when *Sitabo went* to meet their house maids *Rajjo-Sajjo* told her that the parents *Anil and Sunita Vyas along with Tanvi and Yashvi* were extremely shell-shocked due to yesterday's strange evening in which they encountered something very bizarre and fatal. They told that they gives shelter to a girl in their house ans she asks for their help for sometime as she has been new to the town and has forgotten her relatives house after 1 hour or something one of her family member, relative will come and escort her from *Mansa Devi, Vyas Bhawan.*

The family agreed to let the girl who introduces herself as *Noorie to* stay in their house for some hours. She told them that she is a computer operator by profession and can repair any disease regarding the software of the computer device. They offered her tea and pakoras but she denied it as she claims that she is full with parathas and achaar inside her tummy sometime back. But still they insisted her to take atleast some food and if nothing else works then atleast have some fruits. After lot of persuasion she accepted 2 oranges to be eaten by *Noorie. Anil, Sunita and Tanvi Yashvi* asks *Noorie to rest fro sometime after finishing her oranges if she feels tires and later they went inside to do some* work and strangely all went to sleep and after taking a nap when they came out they saw two men inside their house who tries to steal the items from their house and has given them some drugs by their skills in tricking others. They spiked the tea very connivingly when all went inside their rooms for some work. The girl *Noorie* has gone invisible somewhere adn in her place two people were stealing the goods and decorative items from the drawing room hall of the *Vyas family*. The father took a firm decision by calling the cops immediately by dialling 100 no. from the help of a neighbour by going outside the house as the thieves have closed the door of the hoise by a padlock but *Mr. Anil Vyas* who got out of his drugged sleep hear the voice of *Chitti ji his neighbour on his platform and* calls him as a part of outside view is visible from the house.

Thankfully *Chitti ji hear his calls and* called the cops by dialling 100 phone number in the cop station immediately to prevent further damage of the family. The nearby police cell was informed at once and they came to rescue the family and the neighbours too break the door in order to help the needy family in the crises time. The family was rescued by the entrance and the joint union of the helpful and great neighbourhood of *Mansa Devi Gali , respect is the only word for them and* hats off for their efforts, for this they all deserve an applause. The police came on time and the culprits were arrested. It was discovered that the two men were professional conmen who are expert in creating disguise and changed themselves as chameleons. The two were the most wanted criminals who are in the most wanted list of thugs and criminals of the highest order by the Indian police. After the family gets comfortable and normal from the traumatic incident that took place in their life in those 5 hours or something suddenly *Yashvi* encountered robes of a female that was lying down on the sofa set where *Noorie was sitting and sipping her tea and also chatting with the family. This indicates that the thief has* disguised as a cross-dresser, that simplifies the thief has done crossdressing as a female to hide his real identity as well as his ulterior motives. The *Vyas family* vows to never help any human again in their life especially a damsel crossdresser in distress. The show of both the puppets *Gulabo-Sitabo gets over with the curtain puts down in the* **Mayuri Puppet Theatre.**

The End...

Storytelling 6.0~ Title- "Reincarnated"...

The Saturday couple _Enna_ and _Dushyant Sarkar_ came up with this story about a student of _Enna Sarkar_ who used to come to her residence for private tuitions of Maths and she is really fond of _Enna_ and her brilliant lectures. Her name was _Pragati Shah_ and she always tells her interesting stories and also expects the same from _Enna in return._ One day _Pragati_ narrated a story about her relative from _Maurena, M.P._ that is her mother _Vandana's paternal house. Pragati's_ mother has a younger sibling named _Garima_ who is a very intelligent and sharp-minded human being be it in academics or any other co-curricular activities she is the best among the rest in every stream. She is a scholarship student throughout her life and also actively takes part in every events. She has also achieved various accolades and awards for being the best student as well as topper of the year awards to her credit. But as they say good times are short lived and that time always comes with an hourglass by its side. The happiness of _Garima was also short-lived as she has been diagnosed with severe health issues such as_ Tuberculosis (TB) and Jaundice that cannot be cured by medication as the health was neglected and when the medication started her time has come to say goodbye to the world and her family as her time limit on the earth has come to an end. _Alas! Garima a bright student, a_ researcher a scholar, a good academician and a brilliantly smart good human being has died due to the health issues she has been facing in an unfortunate state of events.

After this incident _Pragati's_ grandmother, her Nani ji _Sushma Devi ji_ has become depressed and grief-stricken forever since her youngest daughter has passed away. But as they life is uncertain and anything can happen anytime as one has to move on in life in order to be in pace with the chaotic drama known as life. After many years from this unfortunate incident _Sushma Devi Ji's eldest son Kishore Kumar_ had a beautiful daughter from his marriage after 5 years of courtship and the weirdest or the strangest or it is not wrong to call it to be a bizarre part about the birth of the girl child in the family is that the girl resembles a lot like _Garima her late aunt who died due to a miserable death due to fever and health issues as mentioned by her grandmother herself._ As soon as the girl grows up she not only resembles _Garima in her looks and manner but her whole personality is shaping up to be like her late aunt clears the grandmother in the first place._ She was named _Ginishka_ who is an absolute split image of _Garima be it in mannerisms, looks air be it also in her habits. She also calls Sushma ji as Maa instead of Dadimaa that Garima used to call her and she has learnt those things and manners on her own._

Sushma ji has a strong belief that her late daughter _Garima_ has come back to her and has reincarnated back in the family but this time as her grandchild _Ginishka._ Believe it or not but the form believe of the grandmother and the behaviour plus appearance of _Ginishka screaming this very answer. Sushma ji_ often used to say, "meri beti mere paas wapas aa gai hai, maine usse dil se pukara na wo mujhe jaldi chodh gai thi na isiliye wapas aa gai wo mere paas". Well to be honest if you believe in reincarnation stories then it is true but if not then still an unsolved mystic riddle.

The End...

Storytelling 7.0~ Title- 9 O'clock.

The last story in this Saturday meeting was narrated by *Mouli Ganguly* to everyone who was present in the **Mohini Bagh.** This story is about a 22 year old girl named *Charlie Chauhan* from *Sarla Vihar, New* Delhi, India. *Charlie* is very fond of her father *Manoj Chauhan* who is a veterinarian by profession and mother *Sarojini Chauhan* a housemaker. One day *Charlie's* good friend *Randeep Rai* planned to throw a party in a disc and invited many friends to attend the grand and filmy party.

Charlie took permission from her father to attend the party of his good friend *Randeep Rai* who has invited his group of 13 friends on his birthday at the **Joice Club** for celebrating his birthday with his friends and some relatives. *Charlie's father has an undying and* immense faith on her daughter who according to him is a very responsible and a dutiful daughter, therefore he granted her the permission to attend the party but only on one condition that is to reach the house early which is her curfew time to be at the house that is 9 O'clock. *Charlie* promised her father to come at the accurate time as decided but her mother refuses to allow her to be out of the house at such odd time because of the crime cases been reported almost in regular basis. But *Charlie* promised to be in the house at the decided time that is 9 O'clock, even if the party was not stopped by her friends. Finally after long convincing and buttering *Charlie got the permission by her family to attend the* birthday party of her friend *Randeep Rai. She promised to reach her house sharp at 9 p.m. in the night.*

Charlie reached the party venue at 7:05 p.m. and met all her college pals along with the birthday boy. Together they all partied and indulged into merrymaking activities such as dancing, eating, singing. When it was quarter to 8:20 p.m. *Charlie* told *Randeep* that she will have to leave the party venue as she has promises her father to reach the residence at 9 O'clock sharp. *Randeep Rai* asks her to wait for some more time as he himself will drop her to her house residence but they will leave the venture after 9:00 p.m. But *Charlie* always obeys her father's commands and requests as her father has an immense faith on her and she does not want to break that firm believe and faith that she has gained by her loyalty and trustworthy attitude. She told her friend birthday boy *Randeep Rai* that her father has even fought with her mother to make her attend this party and now it is her time to payback; return that trust and grateful attribute. Saying this she left the venue by assuring him that she will go on her own to her house that is *Tulsidas Enclave house no.28/65, New Delhi. She will catch a passenger vehicle that is through a private CNG auti-ricksahw for reaching out to her house residence.*

After this she came out of the birthday venue and it 8:35 p.m. she took an auto-rickshaw to reach her destination that is **Tulsidas Enclave** *where she resides. Charlie* told the auto-wala bhaiya to take th route of **Tulsidas Enclave, Nalband Road** *and the auto driver fixes the auto ride with* ☐*200.* She settled inside the auto and talked to her parents that she is coming home but en route the auto was stopped due to a minor problem, when the problem was fixed the autowala continued driving the four wheeler vehicle. But suddenly towards the *Khandari Road* another passenger sits in the front side at the left corner of the auto driver. The autowala bhaiya told *Charlie that the passenger is his brother and he needed to reach Dhaakran Chauraha as soon as possible and i*t will not take much time as the route is in the way of *Nalband Road* only said the auto-rickshaw driver. *Charlie* agrees and allows the passenger to sit and asks the autowala to reach as fast as possible as she is getting late. The autowala assured her that she will reach the ***Tulsidas* Enclave** at the right time.

After sometime the autowala took the wrong path towards the empty and isolated *Shamshabad Road* that is a wrong direction. *Charlie* started shouting and screaming for help but there is no one to listen to her agonising distressed calls. She started wailing with fear and anger but there is no one to listen to her gory saga. The auto was stopped at an alienated location towards a desolated & ruined house at *Kuluru, Shamshabad Road.* They forced themselves upon *Charlie and one by one both the men autowala driver and the other men pretending to be a pa*ssenger raped her brutally without showing any mercy on her by full force and monstrosity. They destroyed her completely and not only ruined her body but as well as tormented her soul too in that night full of unknown darkness and unexpected turn of events. While the perpetrators were drinking alcohol, consuming bidhees (desi cigarettes) and playing cards outside the desolated and ruined building where they had gang-raped and sexually molested and harassed the poor victim *Charlie* again and again. She saw the two men breaking her phone and removing her SIM out of the phone and they broke that as well. When she tried to run away from the spot secretly without *the* knowledge of the two rapists but she was caught by them and they ran behind her in order to catch her on time to kill her forever so that she won't register any police case on them for the heinous crime and sin they had committed on her self-esteem and gruesome, horrendous deed of forcing themselves on *Charlie to have sex against her will.* She ran with fear and shiver in her eyes and physical body to save her from the cruel and wicked rapists and perpetrators. The poor girl called out his father at the perilous time.

Dr. *Manoj Chauhan* just woke up from his sleep with an intuition of some unknown and dangerous feeling that his loved one is in deep pain and anguish. It was 9:30 p.m. but their daughter had not returned back and her phone is also switched off when her tried calling *Charli*e. The sadistic serial killer and rapists does nit release the innocent victims even after satiating her must from her by snatching away her self-respect and life. They are even ready to end her life in order to save their lives bloody cowards and hypocrites. Finally when it was quarter to 10:00 p.m. and still the phone of *Charlie* remained unavailable to respond her father and mother went to the police station but all invain as the police has a opinion that the girl will return back as they were if the opinion that she must have stayed late at the birthday party venue but *Charlie's* father was damn sure that his daughter never lies or breaks his promise she must be in some great trouble and anxiety as he can sense it by his senses and his gut feeling is telling him that something really destructive and wrong has happened with his only daughter *Charlie Chauhan.* They even tried calling her friend *Khushboo Shah* who told him that *Charlie* has left the party venue at 8:24 p.m. to reach to her residence at the right time as she has promises and committed her father to reach her house on the right and accurate time.

Finally the police started their investigation to search the missing girl *Charlie Chauhan* but to no avail as they failed to search her anywhere. All they got to know is that she has taken an auti-ricksahw from the *Jalkamal Road where the Joice Club the party venue is situated.* But nothing gets clarified as nobody was sure which auto she has chosen and went towards the *Nalband Road* for her house. Many days have passed but nothing is found out about the whereabouts of *Charlie Chauhan, days have passed into months and months have passed into almost 6 m*onths but nothing was revealed about the girl after almost 9 months or so a news came out that towards the *Monarika district's Kuluru, Shamshabad Roa*d's under construction ruined building a dead body of two auto drivers were located and reported to the cop station.

It was reported that the modus-operandi was some in both the crimes as both the man's private part that is penis was removed from their body and in the post-mortem it was revealed they they were strangled from their necks they were not able to breathe and died due to deficient supply of oxygen and the cause of their deaths were asphyxia and were thrown down from the 5th floor in that state. Their CNG auto was spotted some 20 miles away from their death location towards *Saket Nagar, New Delhi. The place is full of alcohol bottles and cigarettes. A girl from there is spotted saying that those two men tried to rape her but something* mysteriously happened and all of a sudden both the hooligans and scoundrels were out to death in a single gush of air by some strange and mystical couple of events such as the rapists were hanging into the air without any gravitational force and then they died a miserable death and a painful death. This case was also not solved by the police as the murderer was never found out in the open to resolve this death mystery and finally the case is shut due to lack of evidences and no substantial proofs or witnesses, as if the murderer has got vanished into the thin air.

One day suddenly at around 9 O'clock the doorbell of *Dr. Manoj Chauhan rang at the* **Tulsidas Enclave**. When he opened the door an auto wala driver was asking ☐200 from *Dr. Manoj* by saying that his daughter Charlie has told him to wait outside as she will bring 200 bucks from her father but didn't returned back from her house to give his money. "Please give me ☐200 and release me, let me go Sahib"... The doctor looked at the auto driver with strange thoughts and a question mark on his forehead. He was not been able to understand the whole matter as it is so perplexing but suddenly every blurred and flabbergasting thing got clear and a sign of enlightenment and a presence of an entity is understood and perceived by *Dr. Manoj Chauhan Charlie's loving father. He hears the* sound of the door of *Charlie's room* that got open on its own without anyone's support or any sign of air coming inside and he can sense a supernatural & a paranormal presence of his daughter *Charlie* inside the house who has promised her father to reach the house on the 24th of September, 2010 on time sharp at 9 O'clock and the bizarre thing about the whole incident is that it was quarter to 9.00 p.m. on the wall clock. This was Dr. *Manoj Chauhan's ultimate enlightenment and wisdom of her presence inside the house and the promise that she has kept of her father to be at the house sharp at 9 O'clock.*

The End...

This also marks the end of a wonderful and bizarre way of retelling some infamous and supernatural ghost stories at the deserted location of **Mohini Bagh** *by a group of some social media friends...*

05-12-2019.

12:47 p.m. IST. Online Print.

<u>Epilogue:-</u>

In the hope of creating my own niche, my own liberal thoughts and visions I'm presenting some of short stories to all the divine readers, some of which are based on the societal issue while some are simply hilarious and mind-boggling. The ultimate purpose of the excogitation of these tales is to delight the readers and also to admonish them for the ethical code of conduct. Even if I reach just 10% of what I have expected from my liberal visions and thoughts then I will believe that I have finally succeeded in my mission of entertaining my readers along with enlightening them with my collection of stories. Until then *"Sink yourself in the world of Sweekriti"... Chao Chao.*

© *"S.MANNAH"!!*

(All Rights Reserved).